# Dear Vampa

Written and illustrated by Ross Collins

Hodder
Children's
Books

A division of Hachette Children's Books

Dear Vampa

Copyright © 2009 Ross Collins

First published by Katherine Tegen Books, an imprint of
HarperColllins Publishers USA, 2009

First published in the UK in 2010 by Hodder Children's Books

This paperback edition published in 2011

Hodder Children's Books, 338 Euston Road, London, NW1 3BH

Hodder Children's Books Australia, Level 17/207 Kent Street, Sydney, NSW 2000

The right of Ross Collins to be identified as the author and illustrator
of this Work has been asserted by him in accordance with
the Copyright, Designs and Patents Act 1988.

A catalogue record of this book is available from the British Library.

ISBN 978 1 444 90021 7

Printed in China

Hodder Children's Books is a division of Hachette Children's Books.

An Hachette UK Company.

www.hachette.co.uk

For Eunice

To: Vampa
    The Ruined Abbey
    Lugosi Lane
    Transylvania

From: Bram Pire
    66 Nostfer Avenue
    Harkerville
    Pennsylvania

Dear Vampa,

    Sorry for not writing for so long, but we've been having some trouble with our new neighbours.

They are called the Wolfsons.

They moved in three months ago with an **awful** lot of weird stuff.

They invited us over for a "housewarming".

There was **nothing** for us to drink at all.

# The Wolfsons stay up **all** day long.

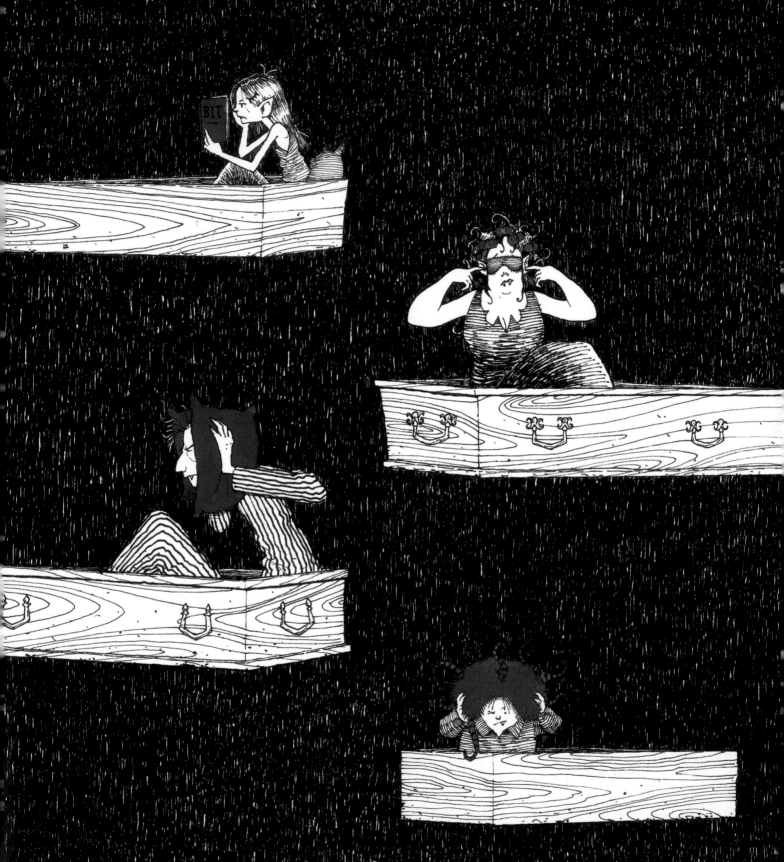

We haven't had **any** sleep in weeks.

They have a bizarre fondness for sunshine.
Mum says it's disgusting.

The Wolfsons tend to lock their windows every night.
It's **SO** inconsiderate.

Last month they invited us
to a Halloween party.

It wasn't much fun.

Their unpleasant pet
doesn't seem to warm to us.

And they don't seem
to like Cuddles either.

Things came to a head on Wednesday.

We all went out for our evening flutter,
and the Wolfsons shot us out of the sky.

Mum doesn't think she'll be able to face flying again.

Dad says he has had enough.
He used some **very** bad words.

As I write, we are moving out. We are coming back to Transylvania to stay with you for a while.

Mum asks if you can get the guest crypt ready for us.

Hope this finds you unwell. All my love to Vampma.

Lovebites,

Bram x x x

"It's so hard to find good neighbours."